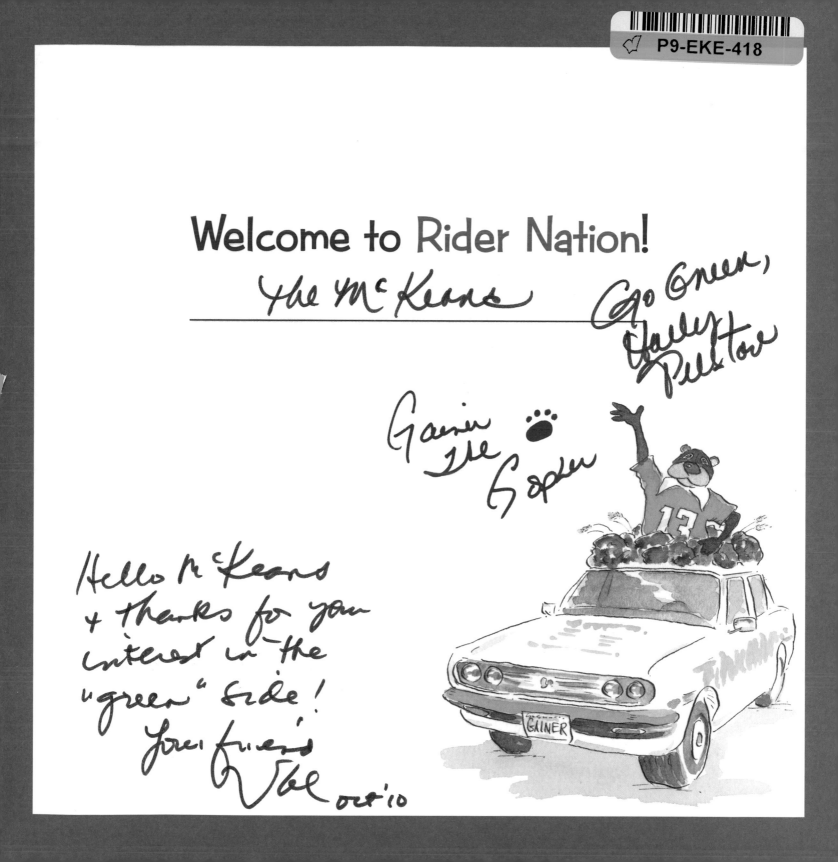

Welcome to Rider Nation!

The ALWAYS Team

Written by Holly Preston
Illustrated by Val Lawton

Your Nickel's Worth Publishing

The Always Team

Text © 2010 Holly Preston
Illustrations © 2010 Val Lawton

Manufactured by Friesens Corporation in Altona, MB, Canada
September 2010
Job #58216

Library and Archives Canada Cataloguing in Publication

Preston, Holly
        The always team / Holly Preston ; Val Lawton [illustrator].

ISBN 978-1-894431-51-4 (bound).

        1. Saskatchewan Roughriders (Football team)--Juvenile fiction. I. Lawton, Val, [date]- II. Title.

PS8631.R467A78 2010   jC813'.6   C2010-905187-4

Design by Heather Nickel

With many thanks to the Saskatchewan Roughriders for their cooperation and support.
And a high-five to Imagine Marketing for helping make this book a reality.

Your Nickel's Worth Publishing gratefully acknowledges the Government of Saskatchewan, through the Creative Economy Entrepreneurial Fund, for its financial support.

Saskatchewan
Ministry of
Tourism, Parks,
Culture and Sport

ENVIRONMENTAL BENEFITS STATEMENT

Your Nickel's Worth Publishing saved the following resources by printing the pages of this book on chlorine free paper made with 10% post-consumer waste.

TREES	WATER	SOLID WASTE	GREENHOUSE GASES
1 FULLY GROWN	539 GALLONS	33 POUNDS	112 POUNDS

Calculations based on research by Environmental Defense and the Paper Task Force. Manufactured at Friesens Corporation

FSC
Mixed Sources
Cert no. SW-COC-001271
© 1996 FSC

imagine
marketing

Your Nickel's Worth Publishing
Regina, SK.

www.yournickelsworth.com

For all young Rider fans who know that football helmets
really do grow from watermelon seeds

Brendan had **ALWAYS** loved playing football.

But he didn't like losing …

… and his team was losing more than it was winning.

Rob, Stevie and Brendan were the Rae Street Riders.
They knew there had to be a way to turn their season around. But how?

Rob, the offensive lineman, said, "We should get a new receiver."
Stevie, the receiver, said, "We should replace our lineman."
Brendan thought they should definitely keep the quarterback.

"Why don't you do what the Saskatchewan Roughriders do?" asked Gramps. "They **ALWAYS** figure it out. We don't call them the **ALWAYS** Team for nothing." "What do the Riders do?" asked Brendan.

"Why don't we find out?" suggested Gramps.
"Boys, there's a Rider game tomorrow and we're all going!"
Gramps never missed a Rider game. He'd been a Rider fan forever.

This was their chance to find out what Gramps meant
when he called the Riders the **ALWAYS** Team.

Brendan and Rob and Stevie still weren't certain they'd find the clues to their losing football season at the Rider game. But early in the first quarter it started to become clear: Gramps called the Riders the **ALWAYS** Team because ...

The players **ALWAYS** look fierce and determined.

The fans **ALWAYS** show their Rider Pride.
And green is the colour, **ALWAYS**.

Gainer is **ALWAYS** the biggest, most hilarious gopher ever.

The Riders **ALWAYS** try to win — but don't **ALWAYS**.
And Rider fans know there's **ALWAYS** next year.

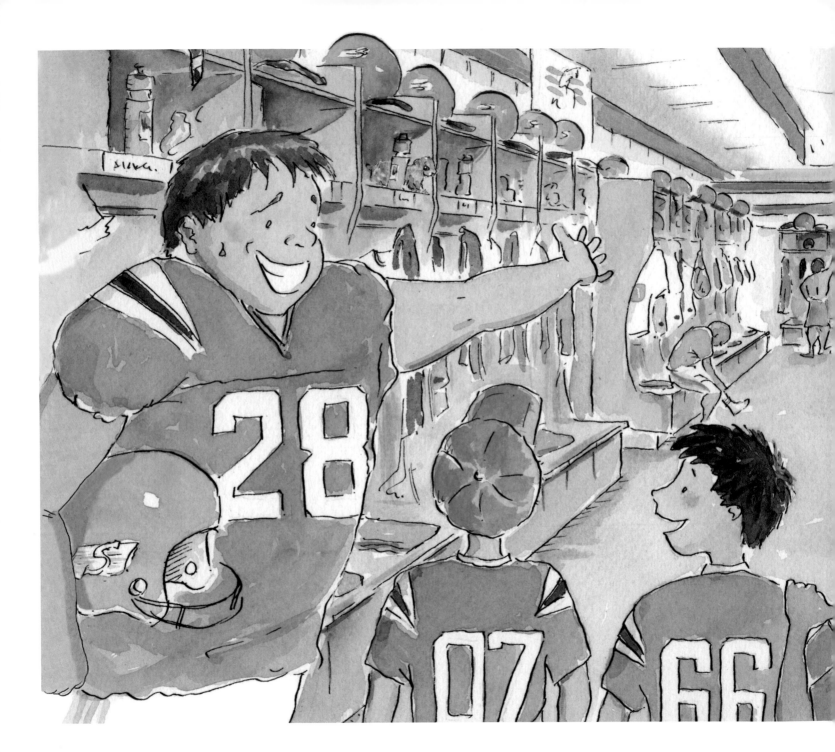

The boys were excited after the game. Rob's favourite player
even stopped to talk to them. "Guys, want to meet the team?" he asked.
Brendan and Rob and Stevie stared up at the players.

The Riders hung up their football uniforms. They put away their helmets and cleats for another day. The boys asked lots of questions but most of all, they listened. And this is what they learned:

If you ask a Rider, he will tell you winning is important — but also that you **ALWAYS** …
Believe.

Play like a team.

Celebrate only the big plays.

Play tough …

… and with heart.

Have fun.

ALWAYS honour the tradition …

… and **ALWAYS** thank your fans, the 13th man.

The boys decided then and there they wanted to play the way the Riders do.
They could hardly wait to practise tomorrow.

"And you know, boys, there's more," Gramps said on the way home. "In Saskatchewan, if you give a boy a football, he will **ALWAYS** dream about becoming a Rider. And here that's **ALWAYS** possible."

"We already know *this*," Stevie said, "once a Rider fan, **ALWAYS** a Rider fan!"

Gramps nodded. "You got it! One province, one team and **ALWAYS**…
one **GOPHER!**"

Holly Preston

Holly has been a Rider fan since way back when. Thankfully, her parents raised her in a place where green and white and community are words that ALWAYS belong in the same sentence.

She has had a career as a broadcast journalist with CTV and CBC. On the day our team brought the Grey Cup home in 1989, she was lucky to host a TV special from Taylor Field watched by fans throughout Saskatchewan. It's the only time she'll ever get to be on the 50-yard line. How sweet it was!

Today, Holly's two sons wear their Rider colours with pride, just as their grandfathers Ken and Ted would want.

Val Lawton

When you're a little girl growing up on the golden prairies of Saskatchewan, your dreams are as big as the endless swaying wheat fields and the eternal blue sky stretching overhead. For Val, those dreams were filled with simple, yet compelling images of people dotted against a landscape washed with sun.

While Val enjoys creating art for both kids' and grown-ups' books, she also loves working with schoolchildren as an artist-educator with the Royal Conservatory of Canada's "Learning Through the Arts" program.

Val lives with her husband, two kids and a beagle, all of whom cheer for the ALWAYS Team on game day!

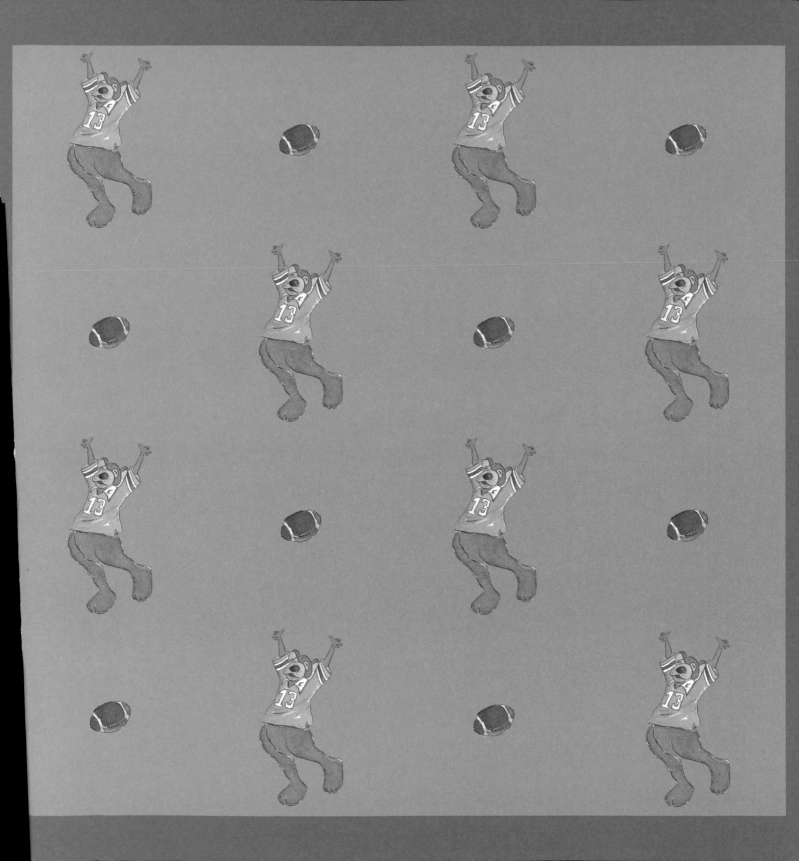